ANOTHER
FISH STORY

Dr. G. F. WELCH

Illustrated by Irina Kostunina

For Liam and Dominic.

I was watching television. It was my favorite program, but I guess they are all my favorite. Papa told me to turn the television off so that we could do something else. He wasn't watching me so I stuck my tongue out at him.

He got mad and said, "Dommy, don't do that. It's so ugly."

So, Papa took me to the pond. He wanted to show me what fish looked like. We walked and walked and walked but we didn't see any fish. Papa was tired, so we sat down near the water on the grass. Papa is kind of old, so he laid down and fell asleep.

Then, I heard the splashing of the water. A fish splashed with his tail. Then, another fish splashed with his tail too. Now, a lot of fish were splashing.

Papa was still asleep. Then, one big fish stuck his head out of the water and looked right at me. He winked one eye at me. I motioned to him to come to me. I was not going to go out in the water to him. He swam real fast right at me and was on the grass in front of me.

I asked him, "What are you?"

He said, "I'm a catfish. See my whiskers?" I nodded. He smiled and then he started flopping. He flopped all the way around me. He flopped all the way around Papa. He flopped until he was in front of me again.

"Would you like to see some other fish?" he asked.

I said, "But you're a fish. You can't talk!"

"Do you want to see some fish, or sit here arguing about it?" he asked.

"Yes," I said. "I would like to see other fish."

Then, another fish stuck his head out of the water and stared at me. The catfish had told him about me. Mr. Cat whistled so he swam really fast and was on the grass in front of me.

I said, "what are you?"

He said, "I'm a trout. See my spots?" I nodded. He said, "I'm also the best and most popular of the fish."

He smiled and then started flopping. He flopped all the way around me.
He flopped around Papa. He flopped until he was in the water again.

Then, another fish stuck his head up. Mr. Cat whistled to him and he swam really fast. He was on the grass in front of me so I asked him, "What are you?"

He said, "I'm a carp. See all my scales, my small whiskers and my long body?" He even let me touch him and feel the scales.

Mr. Carp kept watching Mr. Cat. He seemed to be afraid. Then he started flopping. He flopped by Papa. He flopped by me. He flopped until he was back in the water.

Mr. Cat laughed at Mr. Carp when he was gone. "Did you see how scared he was?" Mr. Cat asked. "I'm the guy who keeps these guys in line and old carpy knows it."

Another fish stuck its head up. This was a girl fish. She was not as big as the other fish. Mr. Cat whistled to her and she came up on the grass to me.

I asked her, "What are you?"

She said, "I'm a perch. See my color and my stripes. I am much prettier than the other fish." She was right about that.

Mr. Cat winked one eye at her. I think he might have liked her.

Then, she flopped, and flopped, and flopped, all the way around Papa and me. When she was back in the water, Mr. Cat whistled again.

Another fish stuck his head up. He winked one really small eye at the girl perch and then he swam up to me. These big fish all seemed to like that pretty perch. Even at the pond, it was all that kissy stuff.

I said, "What are you?"

"I'm a sturgeon," he said. "See my really long body, my pointy head, these lines on the side of my body? I even have this tongue that hangs from my mouth. That's how I find food. I'll be eight feet long when I finish growing. Check out this armor with bony plates."

"Wow," I said, "That's bigger than Papa." I knocked on his armor. It was very hard. Mr. Sturgeon glanced at Papa sleeping on the grass and then winked one eye at me.

"Well, I've got to go," he said. "I'm drying out and that's not a good thing." Then, he flopped, and flopped, and flopped, all the way around Papa and me.

"Well, I'm sure glad he's gone" said Mr. Cat. Do you know that he eats crawdads and snails? That's just so yucky."

Another fish stuck her head up. Mr. Cat whistled to her and she came up on the grass to me.

I said, "What are you?" This was another girl fish. She was about as big as the perch fish.

She said, "I'm a bluegill. See my color and my scales. I have this spiny fin on top. Then there's my beauty mark on the side of my head. I am much prettier than the other fish. I'm even prettier than the perch."

Mr. Cat winked one eye at her. I think he might have liked her too.

Then, she flopped, and flopped, and then Papa snored really loudly. Miss Bluegill stopped and looked at papa. Then she flopped and flopped all the way around Papa and me. When she was back in the water, Mr. Cat whistled again.

Another fish stuck his head up. He winked one really small eye at the girl bluegill and then he swam up to me. These big fish all seemed to like those pretty fish.

I said, "What are you?"

"I'm a pike but some people think I look like a muskie or a gar," he said. "See my really long body, my pointy head, the scales, the yellow bean shaped spots, and these black spots on my fins? I'll be almost five feet long when I finish growing."

"Wow," I said, "That's really big. I bet you could give me a ride."

Mr. Pike just exhaled. "I don't give rides to little boys," he said. He glanced at Papa sleeping on the grass and then winked one eye at me. Then, he flopped, and flopped, and flopped, all the way around Papa and me.

When he was back in the water, Mr. Cat said, "I'm sure glad he's gone. He gives me the creeps. With those teeth he will eat anything, even frogs." Then, he whistled again.

Another fish stuck her head up. She swam up to me.

I said, "What are you?"

"I'm a bass," she said. "See my green body, this line along both sides of my body and how my upper lip sticks out farther than my lower lip? Us girl bass are bigger than the boys. I'll be thirty inches long when I finish growing."

"Wow!" was all I could say. That green color sure made her look pretty.

"Alright, move along," said Mr. Cat. Then, she flopped, and flopped, and flopped, all the way around Papa and me. Mr. Cat said, "She's such a bragger." Then, he whistled again.

Another fish stuck his head up. He swam up to me and just stared at me. Then, he said, "Well, did you want something?"

I said, "What are you?"

"I'm a crappie," he said. "That's crop eee. I usually sleep during the day so that I can look this good. I don't get very big but when you're this good looking, you don't need to be large."

All that I could think of to say was "Well, alright then. Get along now." Then, he flopped, and flopped, and flopped, all the way around Papa and me.

Another fish stuck his head up. He swam up to me.

I said, "What are you?"

"I'm a walleye," he said. "That catfish saved the best, that's me, for last. He has real class! See my long body, my scales, my different colors, and my sharp teeth?"

"Wow," I said, "Those are sharp teeth!" Then, he flopped, and flopped, and flopped, all the way around Papa and me. He also made a lot of noise.

Then, Mr. Cat said, "That is one bad dude."

Then, Papa started to wake up. Mr. Cat said, "I have to go now. I was getting dry anyway."

"Wow!" Papa said. "I guess I was tired. I hope you weren't bored. I'm so sorry you didn't get to see any fish."

"Oh, but I did see fish and I made so many friends! First Mr. Catfish came up to me. Then, he told me who he was. Then he introduced his friends. They were all very nice and wonderful to see."

Papa said, "Now Dommy, you know fish can't really talk."

"But Papa, they did! I told Mr. Cat that he couldn't talk, but he just ignored me."

Papa said, "Well, at least they didn't stick their tongues out. We still need to talk about that."

Since he wasn't watching the water, the fish all smiled at me and stuck their tongues out.

ope you enjoyed this story. I would also appreciate your comments in an Amazon review. Your comments determine
 future of this book, absolutely! I may do follow up stories using the characters in this book, but only if you would
 for me to. I do read all comments so please, please, please take the time to do a review. Thanks!

CPSIA information can be obtained
at www.ICGtesting.com
Printed in the USA
BVHW021929051021
618129BV00022B/496

9 781087 909998